W9-CKT-784
DISCARD

AFTER HAPPILY EVER AFTER

Jack and the Bean Snacks

First published in the United States in 2009
by Stone Arch Books
151 Good Counsel Drive, P.O. Box 669
Mankato, Minnesota 56002
www.stonearchbooks.com

First published by Orchard Books, a division of Hachette Children's Books.
338 Euston Road, London NW1 3BH, United Kingdom

Library of Congress Cataloging-in-Publication Data
Bradman, Tony.
[Jack's Bean Snacks]
Jack and the Bean Snacks / by Tony Bradman; illustrated by Sarah Warburton.
p. cm. — (After Happily Ever After)
Originally published: Jack's Bean Snacks. London: Orchard Books, 2005.
ISBN 978-1-4342-1305-1 (library binding)
[1. Moneymaking projects—Fiction.] I. Warburton, Sarah, ill. II. Title.
PZ7.B7275Jac 2009
[Fic]—dc22 2008031832

Summary: Jack is ready for another adventure, but what could be as exciting as tricking the giant and stealing the golden goose? A trip to the local forest superstore gives him some food for thought. Find out if Jack can gain his mother's trust with his new plan.

Creative Director: Heather Kindseth
Graphic Designer: Emily Harris

1 2 3 4 5 6 14 13 12 11 10 09

Printed in the United States of America

After Happily Ever After

Jack and the Bean Snacks

by Tony Bradman
illustrated by Sarah Warburton

STONE ARCH BOOKS
www.stonearchbooks.com

So Jack defeated the giant,
grabbed the golden goose,
and lived happily ever after
with his mother.
And then ...

"Come on, Jack," said Mom. "Up the stairs and into your pajamas, please. It's time for bed. And don't forget to brush your teeth."

"But it's only seven o'clock!" cried Jack. "And do you have to talk to me like that, Mom? I am not a little boy anymore."

"Well, you are to me," said Mom. "Now up those stairs."

"But I'm a hero, Mom," said Jack. "I climbed the beanstalk,

outwitted the terrifying giant,

and got my picture in all the newspapers, remember?"

"How could I forget?" Mom sighed. "It could have been a disaster! You never think things through, Jack. I sent you to sell poor old Daisy the cow because we had no money, and all you came home with was a few beans."

"Magic beans," said Jack. "And everything worked out okay, didn't it? I brought you back a bag of gold, and a hen that lays golden eggs."

"Ha! The gold lasted a week, and that hen only lays an egg when she feels like it, which is about once a month," Mom snorted.

"So we're not as rich as everyone in the forest seems to think," she went on. "I don't get time to sit around watching TV, anyway. Not like some people I could mention."

"You liked the Singing Harp, though, didn't you?" Jack asked.

"Oh, yes," said Mom. "Until I discovered it sings the same song over and over again!"

"Now if you're not upstairs by the time I count to five," she said.

"I'm going," Jack grumbled.

Later, Mom came up to check that Jack had brushed his teeth and give him a bedtime kiss.

Jack lay in bed, unable to sleep, wondering what he could do to make Mom treat him differently.

He remembered what she'd said about not having time to sit around, and suddenly he felt guilty. Perhaps if he helped her more she would feel better.

When Jack came down to breakfast the next morning, he heard his mom muttering.

"There just aren't enough hours in the day," she said. "How can I go to the supermarket and get the laundry done?"

"Don't worry, Mom," said Jack. "I'll do the shopping for you."

"I don't think so," Mom said, shaking her head. "What's brought this on, anyway?"

"I'd just like to help you," said Jack, giving her a big smile. "And couldn't you tell me what to do? I mean, it can't be that hard, can it?"

"All right, then," said Mom. "Here's the list and some money. It's more than you'll need, so I expect to see plenty of change. Come straight back from the supermarket and don't talk to strangers, okay?"

"No problem, Mom," said Jack. "You can trust me."

At the supermarket, Jack grabbed a cart and quickly made his way to the fruit and vegetable section.

Mr. and Mrs. Goldilocks were already there, glumly examining the fruit.

"I'm sick of eating the same things all the time," said Mr. Goldilocks. "They don't have much variety here, do they?"

Jack looked around. He had to agree. So he moved on to the next section without picking up anything, even though fruit and vegetables were the first items on Mom's list.

He scanned the rest of the list and frowned.

None of it was very exciting. What Mom needed was a little treat to cheer her up. A couple of big tubs of Double Chocolate Chip ice cream should do the trick.

Half an hour later, Jack's cart was overflowing with treats of all kinds—ice cream, candy bars, chips, cookies, cupcakes, and bottles of soda.

He had spent all of the money, and he hadn't bought anything that was on Mom's list. When he got home, Mom was very, very angry with him.

"What have you done?" she moaned. Jack's smile vanished. "We can't live on stuff like this! Besides, I'm trying to lose weight."

"I was only trying to cheer you up, Mom," Jack muttered.

"Well, you've done exactly the opposite," she said. "I'll have to do the shopping all over again tomorrow, and we really can't afford to waste money. So you can go straight to bed without any supper."

That evening, Jack lay in bed, unable to sleep, wondering what he should do. Everything seemed to come back to money. Mom was always worrying about not having enough.

Maybe he should go on another exciting adventure. He could win enough treasure to make them rich for the rest of their lives.

The next morning, Jack came downstairs, ate his breakfast, and acted normal. He was waiting for Mom to leave for the supermarket.

"Goodbye, Jack," said Mom. "Be a good boy while I'm out, okay?"

"What makes you think I'd be anything else?" said Jack, smiling.

Mom rolled her eyes. And as soon as she left, Jack grabbed the hen that laid the golden eggs and ran off. He searched high and low for someone who could sell him more magic beans.

At last, a man listened to him. The man asked about the hen, then smiled.

"Magic beans?" he said. "No problem, kid. I've got loads!"

So Jack traded the magic hen for 100 beans. He had them planted long before Mom got home.

That evening, to Mom's surprise, Jack sent himself to bed early. In the morning, he dashed downstairs. Mom was looking out of the window.

"There you go, Mom," said Jack, proudly. "All of our problems are solved! Well, they will be as soon as I've climbed a few of those huge beanstalks, outwitted some more giants, and won lots of treasure!"

"Huge beanstalks?" asked Mom, puzzled. "All I see is a garden full of ordinary bean plants. Where did they come from? And where's the hen?"

"Oh no! I don't believe it!" moaned Jack, looking out the window. "I've been tricked!"

Of course, Mom was extra angry with him when he told her what he'd done. Now that the hen was gone, they had nothing at all to live on.

"Jack, I know you're trying to help, but when are you going to learn to think before you do anything?" Mom said at last.

And with that, Mom went off to lie down.

Jack trudged into the garden. He was desperate to make Mom change her mind about him. If only he hadn't traded the hen for these tiny bean plants, he thought as he kicked one of them.

A shower of beans fell onto the ground. And suddenly Jack remembered what Mr. Goldilocks had said at the supermarket.

Not enough variety, huh? Well, maybe the supermarket would like to sell beans! He hadn't seen any of them at the store. Jack ran off to get a basket.

Jack did sell his beans to the Forest Superstore. He was very tempted to spend all the profits on a present for Mom, but he didn't. He thought about what she'd said, and he bought a lot more beans instead.

Within a few years, Jack's 100 beanstalks had made him the richest farmer in the forest. He was brilliant at coming up with ideas for new products and outwitting the competition.

His picture was in the papers all the time. And he always thought before he did anything now. So Mom never, ever had to worry about money again.

She was very proud of him. "That's my son!" she would say to all the neighbors, and she let him stay up as late as he wanted. Well, almost.

And so, amazingly enough, Jack and his Mom really did live **HAPPILY EVER AFTER!**

Jacks BEANS
BUSINESS OF THE YEAR
THE END

ABOUT THE AUTHOR

Tony Bradman writes for children of all ages. He is particularly well known for his top-selling Dilly the Dinosaur series. His other titles include the Happily Ever After series, The Orchard Book of Heroes and Villains, and The Orchard Book of Swords, Sorcerers, and Superheroes. Tony lives in South East London.

ABOUT THE ILLUSTRATOR

Sarah Warburton is a rising star in children's books. She is the illustrator of the Rumblewick series, which has been very well received at an international level. The series spans across both picture books and fiction. She has also illustrated nonfiction titles and the Happily Ever After series. She lives in Bristol, England, with her young baby and husband.

GLOSSARY

disaster (duh-ZASS-tur)—an event that causes much suffering

grumbled (GRUHM-buhld)—to speak in a grouchy manner

muttering (MUHT-uring)—to speak in a quiet, low way

outwitted (out-WIT-id)—someone who is outwitted has been fooled

profits (PROF-its)—the money left over after the cost of running the business is subtracted

tempted (TEMPT-id)—to appeal strongly to

trudged (TRUHJD)—walked slowly

vanished (VAN-ishd)—disappeared

variety (vuh-RYE-uh-tee)—a selection of different things

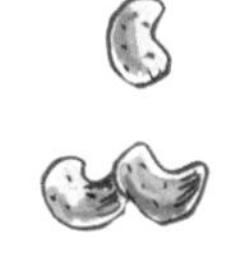

DISCUSSION QUESTIONS

1. Jack trades the goose for magic beans. If you could have a magic vegetable or fruit, what would it be? Why?
2. When Jack notices his mom is stressed, he helps around the house. Discuss what you do to help your parents or friends.
3. At the end of the story, Jack's mom is proud of him. Jack is proud of himself as well. Discuss a time when you felt proud.

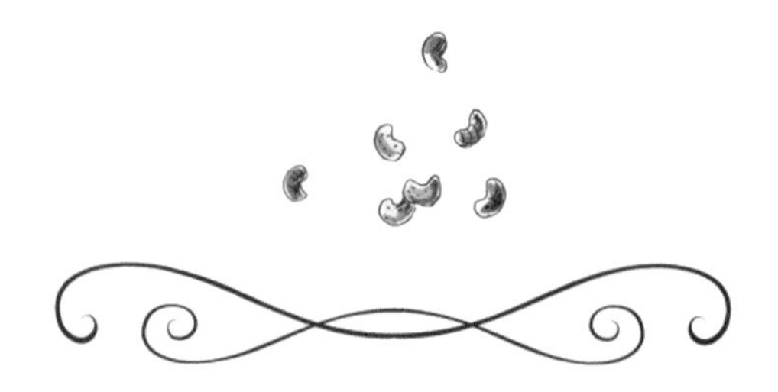

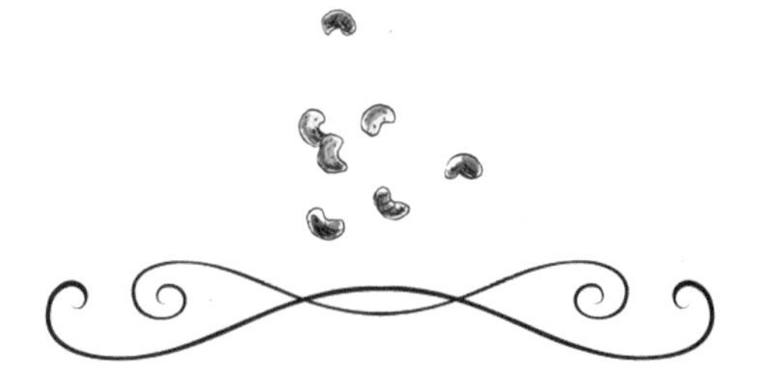

WRITING PROMPTS

1. Jack has a crazy adventure with a giant. Write about a crazy adventure you would like to go on.

2. Jack grows and sells beans to add variety to the grocery store. Write about a product you would like to sell.

3. Jack ends up with a successful bean business. Write a newspaper article about Jack's bean business. Be sure to include quotes from his mom and the giant.

Before there was **HAPPILY EVER AFTER,**
there was **ONCE UPON A TIME ...**

GRAPHIC
SPIN

The Graphic Novel
Hansel and Gretel
retold by Donald Lemke
illustrated by Sean Dietrich
STONE ARCH Fairy Tale
CINDERELLA
The Graphic Novel
retold by Beth Bracken
STONE ARCH Fairy Tale

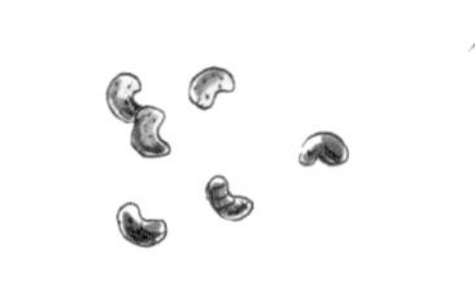

INTERNET SITES

Do you want to know more about subjects related to this book? Or are you interested in learning about other topics? Then check out FactHound, a fun, easy way to find Internet sites.

Our investigative staff has already sniffed out great sites for you!

Here's how to use FactHound:

1. Visit *www.facthound.com*
2. Select your grade level.
3. To learn more about subjects related to this book, type in the book's ISBN number: **1434213056**.
4. Click the **Fetch It** button.

FactHound will fetch the best Internet sites for you!